Elena's Adventurezzzz

Lindsay R. Copeland

About the author

Lindsay is an attorney and former adjunct professor. She currently lives in Bronx, NY but was born and raised in Buffalo, NY. She is a member of the New York Cares, volunteer group. She received a certification in cognitive behavioral therapy and is currently working to complete a NLP (Neuro Linguistic Programming) life coach certification. She is a certified Reiki and sound healing practitioner. She enjoys working on projects that inspire her and allows her to share her passion of love, the universe, nature, and adventure.

Lindsay is excited and honored to share her first children's book!

Dedication

This book is dedicated to Elena, my friend/colleague's daughter who thinks sleep is boring; and to all parents, care givers and anyone else who values nap time.

Sleep is boring- I want to play
Sleep is boring? Boring you say?

I say, no way! Sleep is fun and a great
way to play, with so many adventures,
coming our way.
When we sleep we can dream, there's
nothing we can't do.

We can swim with mermaids,

or ride a kangaroo.

Just imagine all the fun things
we can try.
we can run and jump and
swim and fly!

We can do all of that and so much more,
So many different things and places
to explore.

We can sail a boat, or fly a plane,

or meet up with friends and
play our favorite games!

We can have so much fun in our sleep.

We can do anything in our dreams;

like meet up with our favorite sports team.

Nothing is ever what it seems.

Sleep can be as fun as being awake.
we can play with a dinosaur on
top of a cake,

Birthday Girl

We can visit outer space, or run
in the big race.

01

We can build a giant castle
in the sand.

Or go backstage and meet our
favorite band.

I ♥ DMB

So many adventures and
wonders to see.
that doesn't sound very
boring to me!

Sleep isn't boring after all.

Sleep is fun, we can do it all!

Sleep isn't boring, neither is a nap.

Think of all the adventures we can have.

We get to decide how much fun it can be...

I'm feeling sleepy,

please take a nap for me!

Sleep isn't boring after all!